Shadow Work
JOURNAL PROMPTS

Shadow work journal prompts
to help you heal and grow.

We're here because of you.

When you're supporting a small business, you're supporting a dream. Please leave us an honest review on Amazon by scanning the QR code below ❤

I, _____, vow on this day to commit to my personal growth and acceptance. I promise to fill this journal out with an open heart and good intentions. I acknowledge that there are both pure and impure parts to my being, and I choose to embrace and nurture my wounds. I look forward to unveiling my shadows and bringing more light into this world through personal healing.

_____

SIGNATURE

_____

START DATE

_____

COMPLETION DATE

WHAT IS SHADOW WORK?

Shadow work is the process of unveiling and integrating the parts of yourself that have been repressed or abandoned. You can identify your shadow in times where you experience strong emotions like anger, anxiety, sadness, or fear. Your shadow-self comes from the wounded, irrational parts of your personality that tries to protect you from more pain and trauma. The shadow is neither positive nor negative. In fact, confronting and embracing your shadow is how you begin to heal past wounds, trauma, and shift faulty beliefs.

Shadow work is a personal process and should not be taken lightly. Shadow work will help you dig deep and question your beliefs, perceptions of yourself, and your reality. If at any point during your shadow work journey you feel overwhelmed, take a step back to process your emotions and come back when you feel ready to dive back in.

BEFORE YOU BEGIN SHADOW WORK

Before you start your shadow work prompts, make room in your heart for acceptance and healing.

Let go of thoughts and beliefs that arise from the ego.

Give yourself space to be open to receiving the information that your subconscious will reveal.

Make sure the environment you are in is calm, quiet, and safe.

Give yourself credit for committing to this healing and freeing process.

Begin when you feel called and choose a page theme that speaks to you at that moment.

SHADOW WORK IS LETTING GO OF WHO YOU SHOULD BE SO THAT YOU CAN BE WHO YOU REALLY ARE.

JOURNAL PROMPTS

Fear

What would you do if you weren't afraid?
What would your life look like?

Advice to the past

If you could tell your child-self one piece of advice what would it be?

Inferiority

In what areas of your life do you feel inferior to others? Why?

_____

_____

_____

_____

_____

_____

_____

_____

_____

Envy

Who do you envy and why?
What desires are behind your envy?

Tolerating

Write about your self-sabotaging behaviors
and thoughts.
How can you be more gentle with yourself?

Dream Life

What is your dream life? What does the average
day look like in your dream life?

Passions

What are you drawn to?
What are you passionate about?
What stops you from pursuing this?

_____

_____

_____

_____

_____

_____

_____

_____

_____

Parental Influence

What traits, both good and bad, did you inherit
from your parents or guardians?

_____

_____

_____

_____

_____

_____

_____

_____

_____

Energy

When do you feel the least energized?
What drains your energy?
How do you recharge?

Judgment

What do you judge others for?
What do you judge yourself for?

Regret

What is your biggest regret in life?
Why is this your biggest regret?

Boundaries

How important are you to yourself?
Do you set healthy boundaries?
Why or why not?

_____

_____

_____

_____

_____

_____

_____

_____

_____

Childhood

In your childhood, what did you not receive?
How has this effected you?

_____

_____

_____

_____

_____

_____

_____

_____

Persona

What do you wish more people knew about you?
Why do you hold back from showing this
authentic part of yourself?

Inner Voice

Is your inner voice kind or critical?
What does it say to you on an average day?

Discomfort

In what environments do you feel the most discomfort? What about it makes you uneasy?

Change

Do you prefer change or do you avoid it?
How do you react to change?

Self-Soothing

How do you self-sooth?
How do you feel afterwards?

Traits

What traits do you admire in others that you wish
you had in yourself?

Self Image

What do you dislike the most about yourself?
How can you show these parts of yourself love?

_____

_____

_____

_____

_____

_____

_____

_____

Stress

What keeps you up at night?
Why does it keep you up?

Betrayal

Write about a time you felt betrayed as a child.
How did you react?
How does this effect you today?

Self Image

What about yourself do you hide from others?
What do you tell others about yourself?
Is this who you really are?

Confrontation

How do you feel about confrontation?
Why do you feel this way?

Identify Your Fear

What are you afraid of?
What triggers your fight or flight response?
How do you cope with fear?

_____

_____

_____

_____

_____

_____

_____

_____

_____

Personal Change

What are 3 ways you have changed in the past 3 years? Are they negative or positive changes?

_____

_____

_____

_____

_____

_____

_____

_____

_____

Biggest Dreams

What would you do if your biggest dream
happened tomorrow? What would you feel?

Freedom

What does it mean to be completely free?
When do you feel the most freedom?
What stops you from experiencing freedom?

_____

_____

_____

_____

_____

_____

_____

_____

_____

Hurtful Actions

What is the most hurtful thing you've done to someone?

_____

_____

_____

_____

_____

_____

_____

_____

_____

Shadow Work

What does "shadow work" mean to you?
What has shadow work taught you?

_____
_____
_____
_____
_____
_____
_____
_____
_____

Avoidance

What experiences and emotions do you tend to avoid? Why do you think these bother you?

_____

_____

_____

_____

_____

_____

_____

_____

_____

Perception

How do you feel about yourself as a human?
How do you perceive yourself?
How do you think others percieve you?

_____

_____

_____

_____

_____

_____

_____

_____

_____

Self Love

What ways do you show yourself love?
How do you practice self-care?

_____
_____
_____
_____
_____
_____
_____
_____
_____
_____

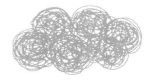

Boredom

What do you do when you are bored?
How do you feel when there is nothing
immediate to do?

Becoming Better

What aspect of yourself would you like to work on? What actions can you take to improve them?

Toxic Traits

Write about your toxic traits.
How do they present themselves?
Do you project them onto others?

_____

_____

_____

_____

_____

_____

_____

_____

_____

Loneliness

When do you find yourself feeling most alone?
When you're surrounded by many people, or
when you're isolated?

_____

_____

_____

_____

_____

_____

_____

_____

_____

Anger

How do you act when you are angry? Is it similar to any people involved in your childhood?

Child-Self

Write about a time you were worried as a child.
What were you worried about?
How did you react?

_____

_____

_____

_____

_____

_____

_____

_____

_____

Social Interactions

Do you often find yourself overthinking what you've said or how you acted in social settings? What usually triggers this?

Overthinking

When do you find yourself overthinking?
What theme of thoughts do you usually
experience when overthinking?

A letter to your future self

Close your eyes and envision your future self. What would you like to say? Write it in a letter format below.

The color of...

What color is pain? Why do you think it is this color? Write about it below.

The color of...

What color is healing? Why is healing this color to you? Write about it below. Think of ways to incorporate this color in your life.

What haunts you?

What is something that haunts you? Think of a
negative recurring thought you have and write
about it below. How can you let this go and
make room for peace?

who loves you?

Think of all of the people in your life that have shown you love. Take some time to appreciate this loving energy and write about it below.

Your life story

If your life was a novel, what would the title be?
Why would it be called this?

Integrating

What have you learned about your shadows?
How can you integrate, accept, and show love
to your shadow self?

A thing in nature

What is the most beautiful thing in nature to you? Is it the mountains or the sea? Is it the stars or a tree? How can you compare this to God?

_____

_____

_____

_____

_____

_____

_____

_____

Made in the USA
Middletown, DE
23 June 2023

33342926R00055